American edition published in 2020

by Andersen Press USA,

an imprint of Andersen Press Ltd.

www.andersenpressusa.com

First published in Great Britain in 2019 by

Andersen Press Ltd., 20 Vauxhall Bridge Road, London SW1V 2SA.

Distributed in the United States and Canada by Lerner Publishing Group, Inc.

241 First Avenue North, Minneapolis, MN 55401 USA

For reading levels and more information, look up this title at www.lernerbooks.com.

Color separated in Switzerland by Photolitho AG, Zürich.

Printed and bound in China.

Library of Congress Cataloging-in-Publication Data Available

ISBN: 978-1-5415-9619-1

eBook ISBN: 978-1-5415-9620-7

1 –TOPPAN–9/1/19

Clem
and
Crab

Fiona Lumbers

ANDERSEN PRESS USA

Clem loved the beach.

The crunch of the wet sand, the crashing of the waves.

The grass that grew sideways as the wind blew in off the sea.

And the pools that came and went with the changing tides.

She would collect the treasures that washed ashore,
but also the things that other people had left behind.

One day, as she was gathering everything
in her bucket, she spied a flash of orange,
then again...

A crab!

The crab watched her as it crawled under, over, and in between the rocks.

But later, as she was ready to head back with her bucket full, Crab had disappeared.

Clem smiled as she told her sister about the crab,
how they'd played hide-and-seek among the rocks.

Together they sorted through her treasures.
One pile to put back, the other to be recycled.

There were shells and pebbles and pieces
of glass that glistened like precious jewels.

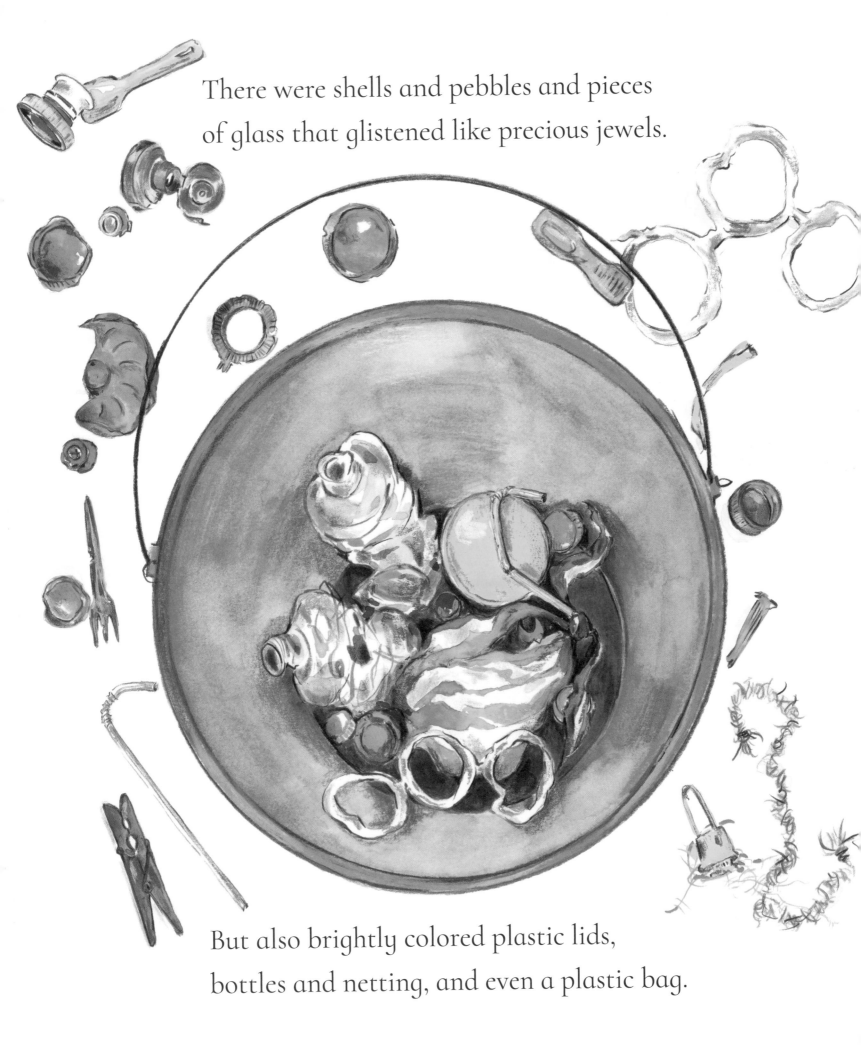

But also brightly colored plastic lids,
bottles and netting, and even a plastic bag.

The bag felt heavy. As Clem looked inside
she glimpsed a flash of orange.

It was Crab—his claw stuck in
the twisted plastic.

Gently she untangled him.

"Can I keep him?" Clem pleaded.

"No, Clem, he belongs in the sea," her sister said.

Sadly, she headed back across
the beach to the pool of water.
Plop! With a small splash, Crab was gone.
"Be careful, Crab," Clem called.

The sun was setting as Clem and her sister caught the bus home.
Clem looked back at the beach and thought of Crab.
"Bye-bye," she whispered.

"Ouch!" Clem felt something nip her leg.

Crab! Somehow he had nestled in her pant leg. She couldn't believe it, as she quickly popped him into her pocket.

"You'll be safe with me," she told him.

Back at home, Clem found a bowl and filled it with seawater and stones from the garden to make a new home for Crab.

Then she took the things she'd collected from the beach to use on her project for show-and-tell.

The following day, Clem and Crab paid a visit
to the aquarium. As they walked beneath
the magical underwater world,
Clem wondered if Crab
missed his home.

They learned lots of facts about
conservation, the huge problem of plastics
in the ocean, and what we can all do to help.

With a head full of facts and Crab carefully hidden in her bag, it was time for Clem's show-and-tell. She told the class all that she'd learned at the aquarium and

explained how her collage was made from the plastic waste she'd gathered from the beach.
"We can all help to protect the oceans and shores. Lots of small actions added together can make a big difference," she explained.

Suddenly, Crab scuttled across the classroom floor!

"Don't be scared," she told her classmates.
"This is Crab, I rescued him from a
plastic bag, his claw was tangled
and he was stuck."

"But why didn't you put him back?" asked Clem's teacher. "I did, but he found me again. The beach is messy and dangerous. I try my best to keep it clean, but it's a big job," she replied.

Clem's teacher smiled and told her that everything she
was doing was great, but that Crab would be much
happier in his natural environment.
Clem knew her teacher was right.
She would have to take him
back to the beach.

That weekend Clem and her sister took the bus back to the beach.

This was usually Clem's favorite time of the week, but today she felt a bit sad …

When they arrived, Clem simply
couldn't believe her eyes!
There, on the sand, were her classmates,
all helping to clean up the beach.

"I made a difference," she called. "We can all make a difference!"
As she skipped across the beach hearing the crunch of the wet sand and the crash of the waves, she was the happiest she'd ever been.

The sunlight danced and glittered on the surface
of Crab's rock pool. With one last glance and a
snap of his claws, Crab was gone.

"I'll see you again, Crab," she called. "Be safe."

Clem felt proud—she'd helped make his home
safe and clean.

This beautiful beach with its endless skies and magical underwater worlds that came and went with the tides; Clem made a promise that she would always look after it—for Crab, and all the other sea creatures.